Written By: Jennifer Brooks
Illustrated By: Lennie Flores

Special Thanks to Stephen Blake Mettee

NADJA Publishing
P.O. Box 326
Lake Forest, CA 92630
714/459-9750 • 800/795-9750
FAX 714/858-3477

1/00

Library of Congress Cataloging-in-Publication Data

Brooks, Jennifer.
Princess Jessica rescues a prince / written by Jennifer Brooks; illustrated by Lennie Flores.
p. cm.
SUMMARY: Princess Jessica welcomes three wise handicapped gnomes to her castle. They tell her of a prince far away whose singing is so beautiful that he was carried off by a lonesome sea serpent. Princess Jessica and her vain sister, Edith, set out to rescue Prince Ryan.
Preassigned LCCN: 93-092628.
ISBN 0-9636335-0-3
1. Self-esteem--Fiction. 2. Handicapped--Fiction. I. Flores, Lennie, ill. II. Title.

PZ7.B766Pr 1993 [E]
QBI93-1001

Printed in Hong Kong
10 9 8 7 6 5 4 3 2 1

For my son Ryan
and the other children of this story.
They live in heaven now,
but continue to teach me about courage,
beauty and love.

Once upon a time, there were two princesses who lived in a castle high above the sea. And although the girls were sisters, they were very different. Princess Edith had long blonde hair and big green eyes, and everyone thought she was very beautiful. And she thought so too. Princess Edith spent hours in front of her mirror with jars of colored makeup and pots with fluffy brushes in assorted sizes. She loved silk and taffeta dresses with lacy ribbons and perfect bows, which she never got dirty, even by accident.

PJ

Her sister, Princess Jessica, called PJ for short, had nice brown eyes and short hair, which she sometimes forgot to comb. PJ spent the mornings caring for the animals on the castle grounds. More than anything else, she loved riding her chestnut pony into the wind, as fast as she could go, without once looking back. When she wasn't outside, PJ was usually in her room reading adventure books and daydreaming of far off places.

In the afternoons, before tea time, the girls would often pretend to have a party. They would dress up, use their best manners, and Princess Edith would practice walking in high heels and crossing her ankles while sitting. She considered this very important, and practiced hard. PJ also liked having parties and wearing her best dresses with fancy french collars. But no matter how careful she was, she always managed to rip a hem or spill jam down the front of them.

One summer day, three traveling gnomes stopped at the castle to rest in the shade. PJ rushed out to welcome them, but her happy smile faded when she saw the littlest gnome of the group sitting in a chair on wheels. She could see he was unable to use his arms or legs, and her heart felt tight with sorrow. She quickly turned her face away so he wouldn't see her cry. But, before the first teardrops fell, the little-boy gnome called out to her.

"Hello, fair princess, my name is Cameron. Want to play ball?"

Startled, PJ looked down into a funny little face with pixie eyes that were wise yet innocent, and a sparkling smile that held just a hint of mischief at the corners. She laughed in spite of herself.

"Hello, Cameron. It's so nice to meet you. Sure, let's play!"

Behind Cameron, tall and solemn, stood an older gnome with great hollow eyes that saw nothing. He was wearing an unusual pendant around his throat.

"This is Geoff," said Cameron. "He has seen much grief and pain in his life and wishes to no longer use his eyes. Instead he sees with his mind's eye. That way, he learns the truths that live in people's hearts."

"Welcome to my home, Geoff," said PJ.

The pendant began to glow brightly. The stately old gnome smiled at the love he saw in Princess Jessica's heart.

Just then the third gnome ran forward and threw her arms around PJ's neck.

"Oh, what a dear lovely girl you are! My name is Jackie. I'm so glad we've found you at last. We were getting very tired."

PJ thought Jackie was delightful even though she had a slightly peculiar look about her, with one eye lower than the other and no hair at all showing beneath her gay bandana. But although Jackie's appearance was somewhat unusual, PJ hugged her tightly. She could see the inner beauty that glowed from Jackie, like a bright star, causing everyone she met to love her.

Taking Jackie's puffy hands in her own, PJ invited her new friends into the castle.

As they served their guests tea and sandwiches, PJ and Princess Edith listened to the gnomes' astonishing tale.

Not long ago, the gnomes' village had held a festival on the cliffs overlooking the ocean. There was much singing and dancing as the gnomes' beloved prince played his guitar and sang for the people. Prince Ryan was adored by all the villagers, young and old alike, for his kindness and gentle loving ways. He didn't care that they were gnomes, or that some were disabled and a few looked less than beautiful to the world. Prince Ryan loved each and every one of them, because they were all special and important to him.

But, as luck would have it, swimming far below was a lonely old sea serpent, who heard the sweet music and desired to have it for his own. It seemed the music touched an empty place in his sad sea serpent soul and made him feel better. So, with his great and mighty tail he grabbed Prince Ryan, guitar and all, and carried him away.

Without Prince Ryan the gnomes felt as though the sunshine was forever gone from their lives. They didn't know how they would carry on without him.

The powerful sea serpent took Prince Ryan to his home at Octopus Garden in the Northern Sea. This island grotto was filled with all sorts of riches and every kind of toy ever made. The sea serpent believed that owning wonderful things would make him happy. He thought playing with beautiful trinkets would keep away the loneliness. But none of his treasures could take the place of having a friend.

The sea serpent insisted that Prince Ryan play and sing for him over and over again, and every time the music played, he would cry. Now sometimes a good cry can make a sea serpent feel better, so he didn't mind the tears. But as soon as the music stopped, the sea serpent remembered he was lonely. Poor Prince Ryan grew weary from all his playing and wondered if he'd ever go home again.

After hearing the gnomes' story, PJ jumped up and called to her servants. "Hurry, everyone, we must go and rescue Prince Ryan!"

As the servants packed, the gnomes approached PJ with gifts and words of advice. Grasping the mysterious pendant at his neck, Geoff spoke for all of them.

"A wise teacher told us when we tired and could travel no more we would find someone who would help us. You are that someone and we thank you from the bottom of our hearts. But you must be very careful crossing the Southern Sea, for mean Lady Sea Serpent lives there. She's had a vile, wicked temper ever since she and Northern Sea Serpent had a lovers' quarrel. They went their separate ways and haven't talked to each other since."

Each of the gnomes handed PJ a small music box to take with her on the journey. "They will help you in times of need," Cameron said.

PJ wondered how music boxes could possibly help her as she carefully wrapped them inside her backpack.

"Remember," said Jackie, "we will be with you in mind and spirit."

"Thank you," replied PJ. "I will do my best to bring your prince home to you."

Just then Princess Edith ran out of the castle with her bags trailing behind her. "Wait! I'm coming with you!" she called. "Once we rescue the prince and he sees my great beauty, he will surely want to marry me!"

So, the princesses and their servants set off toward the Southern Seashore. At the top of the rocky cliffs above the bay, they stopped. Each took a turn peeking over the edge at the sea serpent swimming below. The servants were so frightened by the sight of her that they refused to go any further.

"Edith, we'll just have to go on by ourselves," said PJ. But Princess Edith looked at the angry sea serpent and the steep climb down and said, "But I might rip my pretty new dress! And I'll bet that evil, nasty sea serpent bites princesses!"

"Oh, all right," said PJ. "You can wait here. I'll do it myself." And she bravely started the climb down to the bay alone. She was terribly afraid and felt much too small for such a big task. With each step closer to the bottom, PJ became more and more frightened, until finally she couldn't go on, and sat down to cry.

Suddenly PJ heard music playing. It seemed to be coming from her backpack. She took out the music box Cameron had given her and opened the lid. A glorious melody filled the silent sea air, and PJ recognized Cameron's voice in the music, speaking to her.

"Fear doesn't have to make you weak, Princess. If you stop a moment and reach down deep inside of yourself, you will find the strength and courage you need. Because courage comes from a willingness to be brave even when you're terribly afraid."

Cameron's encouraging words made PJ feel much better. With new-found determination she stood up and held her head high. Without fear she continued on down to the shore. When she reached the water's edge she called to the sea serpent, "Hello! My name is Princess Jessica. May I speak with you a moment?"

Lady Sea Serpent stared at PJ for a while, then she roared, "No! Go away, you foolish little girl! I will not waste one minute of my time on the likes of you!"

PJ heard the angry words and started to feel a little angry herself.

"But I want to talk to you about the sea serpent who lives in the Northern Sea."

"What?" screamed Lady Sea Serpent. "That pig-headed, greedy son of a spotted eel! Leave me alone. I wish not to hear another word about him. You are a silly, bothersome person!"

Now, this made PJ really mad. As a princess, she was almost always very polite. But the sea serpent's refusal to even listen to her made PJ want to scream, throw rocks, and call her the meanest of names!

Before she completely lost her temper, PJ heard another music box playing from inside her backpack. When she pulled it out and opened the lid, she heard Geoff's quiet, patient voice calling softly to her.

"Anger will only lead to more anger, PJ. Instead of getting so terribly furious, why not think of a way to outsmart the hot-tempered lady?"

Well, PJ sat down to think. Since she was a very clever girl, she soon had an idea. "It's too bad you don't want to hear about Northern Sea Serpent," she called out. "I have heard it said that every day he plays songs about his lost love and his broken heart."

"He does?" Lady Sea Serpent swam closer to PJ. "Why, I didn't think he even remembered me! Well, child, what are you waiting for? Let's go to Octopus Garden and see if you're right!"

PJ jumped on the sea serpent's tail and they sailed off toward the Northern Sea. As they neared the grotto, they heard the soft, lovely strumming of a guitar and the words of a tender love song. Lady Sea Serpent was so touched by the ballad she started to cry. Then she rushed into Octopus Garden and threw herself into Northern Sea Serpent's embrace.

"Oh, my sweet, darling love!" she gushed. "Had I only known how you felt about me, I wouldn't have kept you waiting so long. Will you please forgive me?"

Northern Sea Serpent was so surprised by this happy event that he just nodded his head. He was smart enough not to ask questions about his good fortune. "Of course, my dear. Come and be my bride. We'll be together always." The two sea serpents forgot their past grudges and kissed each other gently.

A melody began to play from Jackie's music box inside the backpack. PJ opened the lid and beautiful music filled the grotto. Starting softly and becoming stronger, Jackie's joyous voice sang of a forgiving heart turning hate into love and of love's power to turn sadness into joy.

Crying tears of happiness, Northern Sea Serpent whispered to Prince Ryan. "Go on home now, as you can see I don't need you any more."

The sea serpent gave a high pitched whistle and two playful dolphins jumped out of the water, turning and spinning circles in the sunlight.

"Splish and Splash can take you home," he said.

"Oh, what fun they are!" laughed Prince Ryan. He turned and looked at PJ. "Thank you so much for the rescue, Princess Jessica. You are a very extraordinary girl!"

PJ blushed. "Let's go home, Prince Ryan. Your people have missed you terribly."

Splish and Splash gave the prince and princess a wild roller-coaster ride through the ocean surf. They leaped and frolicked in the waves as their riders laughed and held on tight. As they came near the shore, everyone cheered their arrival.

"Princess Jessica, you are wonderful!" said Prince Ryan. "I have a song the angels have written about you." As the prince played and sang for PJ, Princess Edith came running over. She looked stunning, and was of course perfectly groomed. But Prince Ryan didn't even notice her. He had eyes only for PJ, because when you truly love someone, deeply from the heart, that person becomes the most beautiful person in the world to you. A piece of seaweed stuck in PJ's hair looked to the prince like a golden crown that matched the sparkling flecks of gold in her eyes.

"PJ will you marry me?" asked Prince Ryan. Shyly, PJ hugged him. "Oh, no, of course not, silly," she laughed. "I have many more adventures to make and travels to take!" She smiled at him, and even Princess Edith knew PJ looked beautiful at that moment. "Besides, your people need you to sing and play for them," she said.

"Yes, I know I must go, but you will always be in my heart," said Prince Ryan.

And together, hand in hand, the two friends set off for tomorrow.